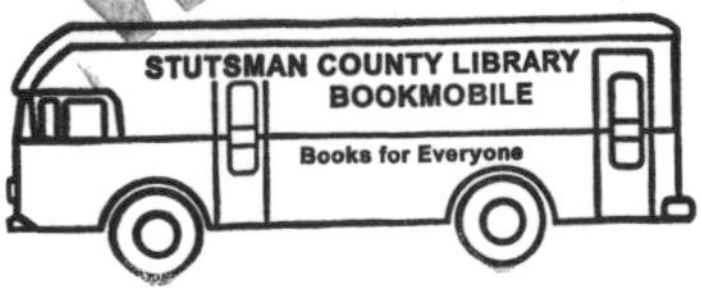
STUTSMAN COUNTY LIBRARY
BOOKMOBILE
Books for Everyone

He trusts no one, and no one trusts him. He appears to serve the Decepticon cause but serves himself first and foremost. Charged with policing the pumps and processors of his fellow Decepticons, he does so with zeal. To him, knowledge is power, and he knows everything there is to know about everyone… except, perhaps, himself! His name…

…IS SOUNDWAVE.

THE TRANSFORMERS: SPOTLIGHT
SOUNDWAVE

WRITTEN BY: SIMON FURMAN

ART BY: MARCELO MATERE

COLORS BY: ROB RUFFALO

COVER ART BY: MARCELO MATERE & NICK ROCHE

LETTERS BY: NEIL UYETAKE

EDITS BY: CHRIS RYALL & DAN TAYLOR

® Licensed by:

Hasbro

Properties Group

Special thanks to Hasbro's Aaron Archer, Elizabeth Griffin, Amie Lozanski, and Richard Zambarano for their invaluable assistance.

Spotlight

VISIT US AT
www.abdopublishing.com

Reinforced library bound edition published in 2008 by Spotlight, a division of the ABDO Publishing Group, 8000 West 78th Street, Edina, Minnesota 55439. Published by agreement with IDW Publishing. www.idwpublishing.com

Library of Congress Cataloging-in-Publication Data

Furman, Simon.
  Soundwave / written by Simon Furman ; art by Marcelo Matere ; colors by Rob Ruffalo ; cover art by Marcelo Matere & Nick Roche ; letters by Neil Uyetake ; edits by Chris Tyall & Dan Taylor. -- Reinforced library bound ed.
    p. cm. -- (The transformers: spotlight)
  ISBN 978-1-59961-477-9
  1. Graphic novels. I. Matere, Marcelo. II. Title.

PN6727.F87S67 2008
741.5'973--dc22

                                                    2007040341

All Spotlight books have reinforced library bindings and are manufactured in the United States of America.

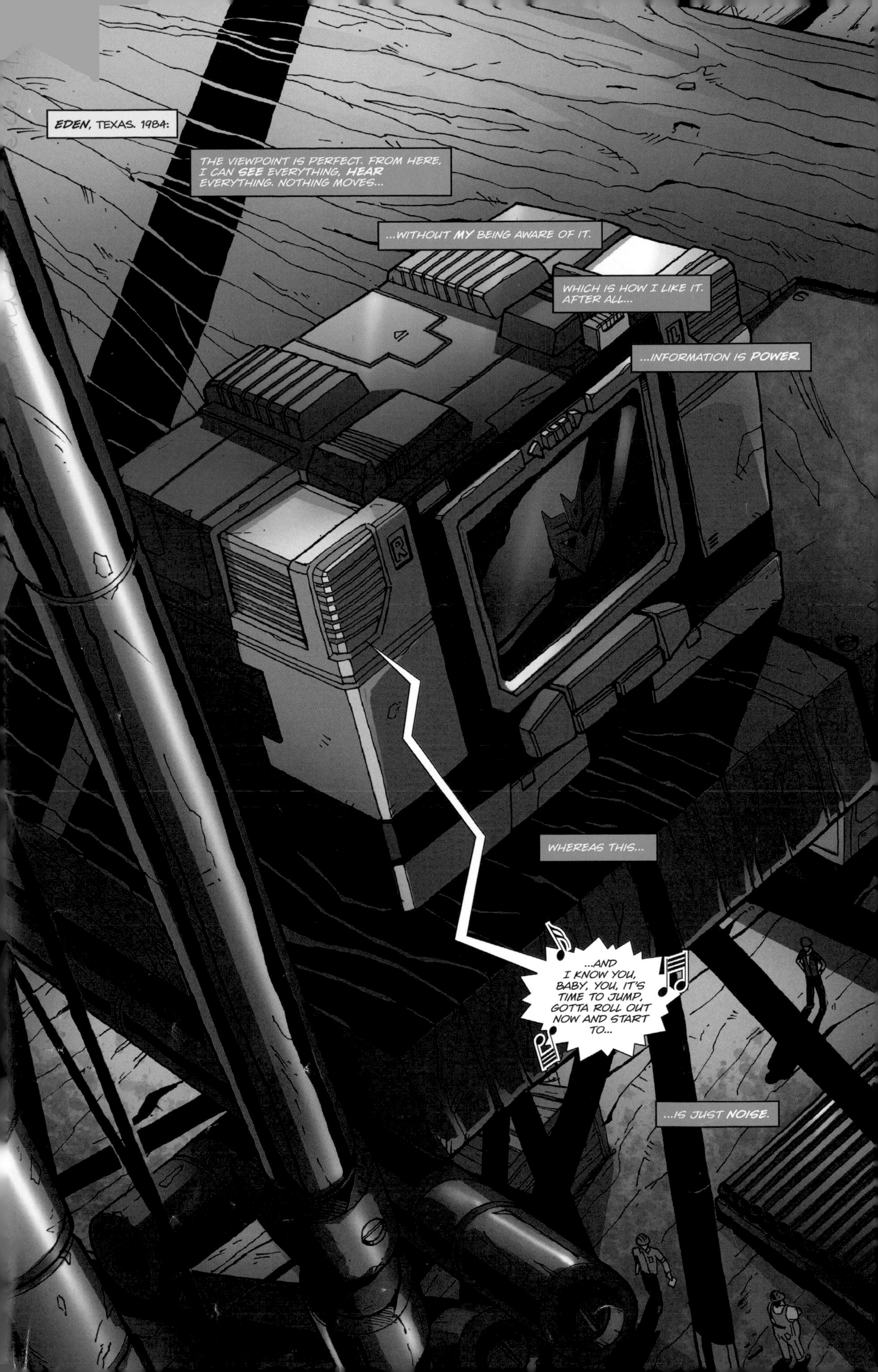
EDEN, TEXAS. 1984:
THE VIEWPOINT IS PERFECT. FROM HERE, I CAN SEE EVERYTHING, HEAR EVERYTHING. NOTHING MOVES...
...WITHOUT MY BEING AWARE OF IT.
WHICH IS HOW I LIKE IT. AFTER ALL...
...INFORMATION IS POWER.
WHEREAS THIS...
...AND I KNOW YOU, BABY, YOU, IT'S TIME TO JUMP, GOTTA ROLL OUT NOW AND START TO...
...IS JUST NOISE.

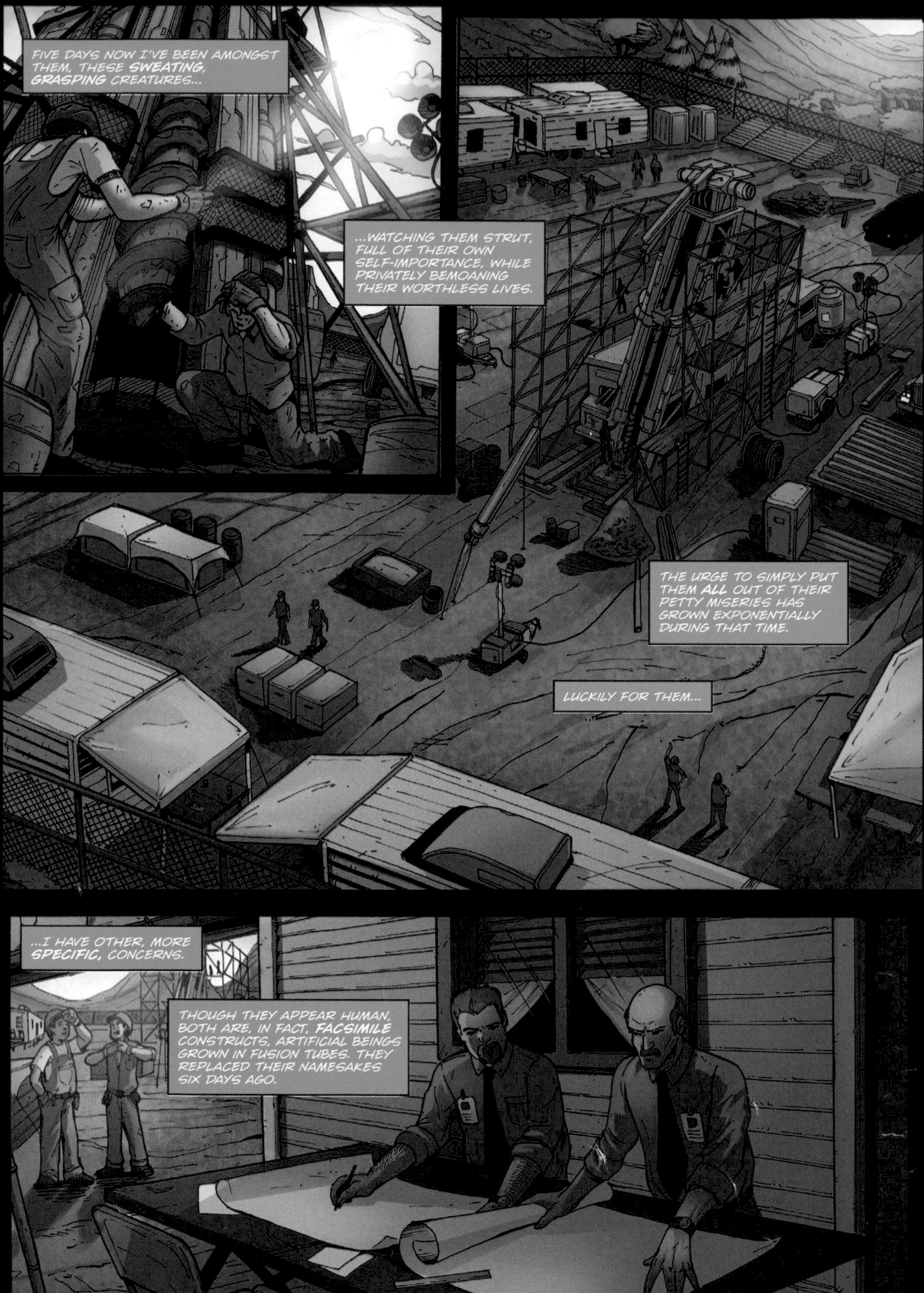
FIVE DAYS NOW I'VE BEEN AMONGST THEM, THESE SWEATING, GRASPING CREATURES...
...WATCHING THEM STRUT, FULL OF THEIR OWN SELF-IMPORTANCE, WHILE PRIVATELY BEMOANING THEIR WORTHLESS LIVES.
THE URGE TO SIMPLY PUT THEM ALL OUT OF THEIR PETTY MISERIES HAS GROWN EXPONENTIALLY DURING THAT TIME.
LUCKILY FOR THEM...
...I HAVE OTHER, MORE SPECIFIC, CONCERNS.
THOUGH THEY APPEAR HUMAN, BOTH ARE, IN FACT, FACSIMILE CONSTRUCTS, ARTIFICIAL BEINGS GROWN IN FUSION TUBES. THEY REPLACED THEIR NAMESAKES SIX DAYS AGO.

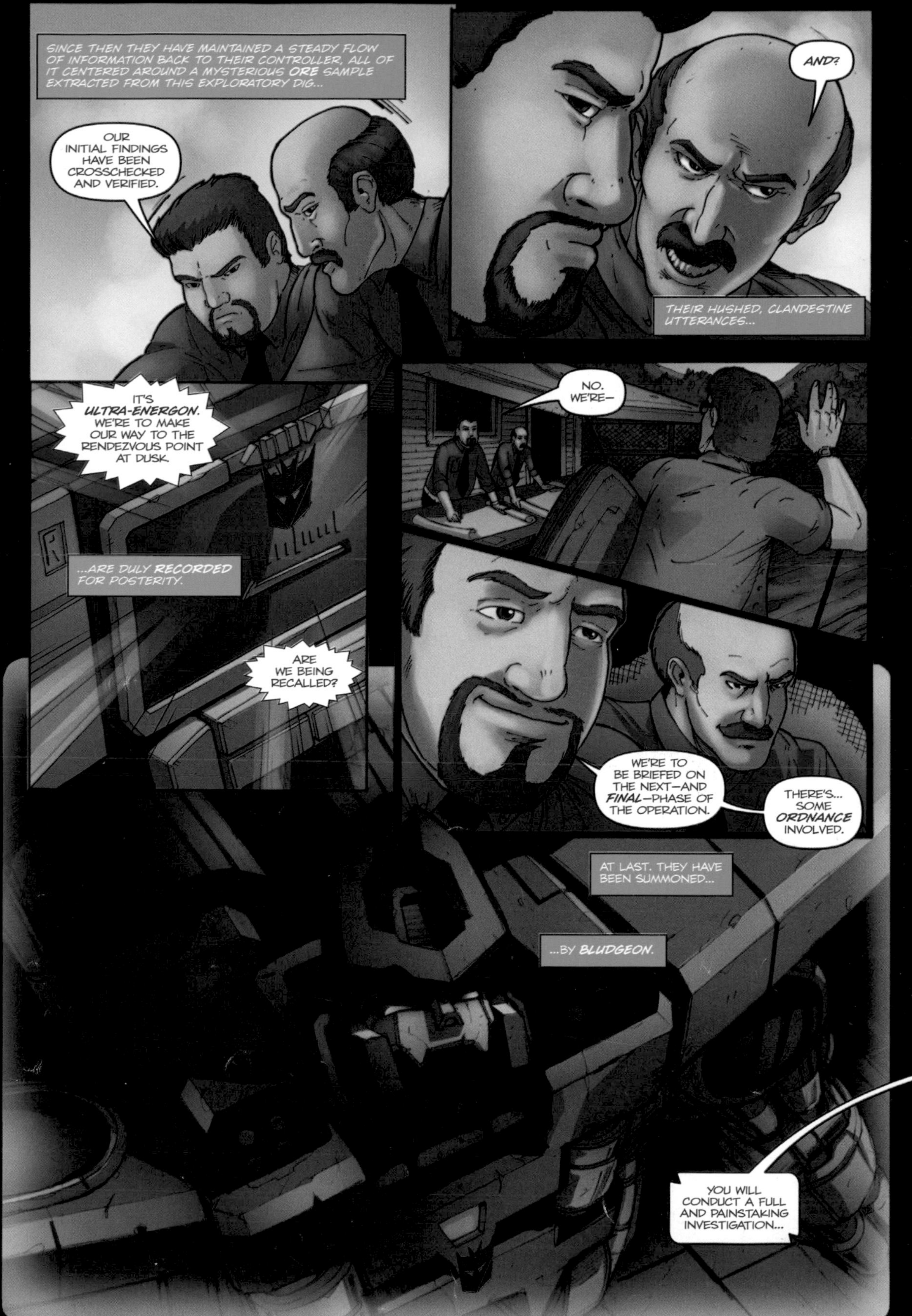
SINCE THEN THEY HAVE MAINTAINED A STEADY FLOW OF INFORMATION BACK TO THEIR CONTROLLER, ALL OF IT CENTERED AROUND A MYSTERIOUS ORE SAMPLE EXTRACTED FROM THIS EXPLORATORY DIG...
OUR INITIAL FINDINGS HAVE BEEN CROSSCHECKED AND VERIFIED.
AND?
THEIR HUSHED, CLANDESTINE UTTERANCES...
IT'S ULTRA-ENERGON. WE'RE TO MAKE OUR WAY TO THE RENDEZVOUS POINT AT DUSK.
...ARE DULY RECORDED FOR POSTERITY.
ARE WE BEING RECALLED?
NO. WE'RE—
WE'RE TO BE BRIEFED ON THE NEXT—AND FINAL—PHASE OF THE OPERATION.
THERE'S... SOME ORDNANCE INVOLVED.
AT LAST. THEY HAVE BEEN SUMMONED...
...BY BLUDGEON.
YOU WILL CONDUCT A FULL AND PAINSTAKING INVESTIGATION...

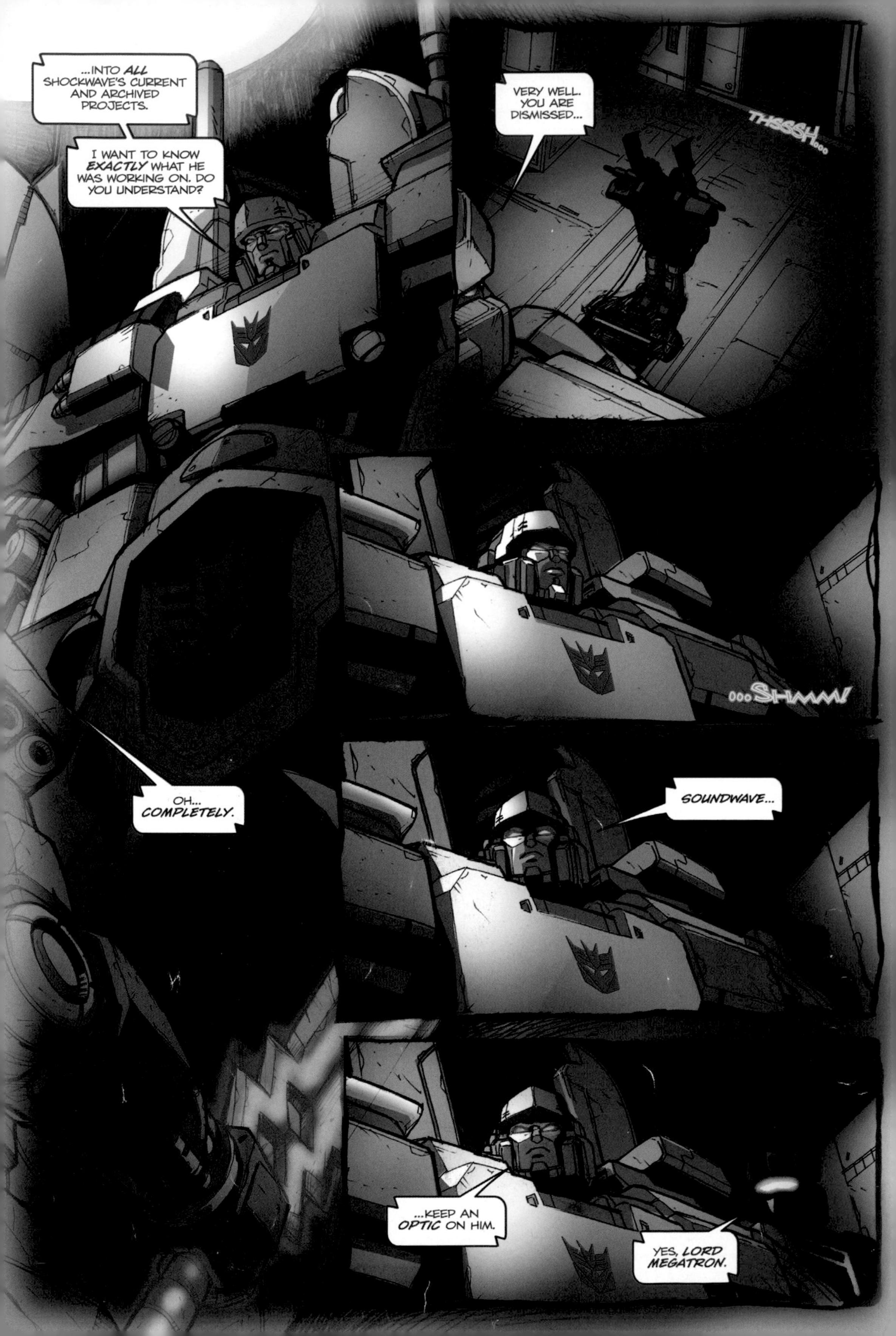

...INTO ALL SHOCKWAVE'S CURRENT AND ARCHIVED PROJECTS.
I WANT TO KNOW EXACTLY WHAT HE WAS WORKING ON. DO YOU UNDERSTAND?
VERY WELL. YOU ARE DISMISSED...
THSSSH...
...SHMM!
OH... COMPLETELY.
SOUNDWAVE...
...KEEP AN OPTIC ON HIM.
YES, LORD MEGATRON.

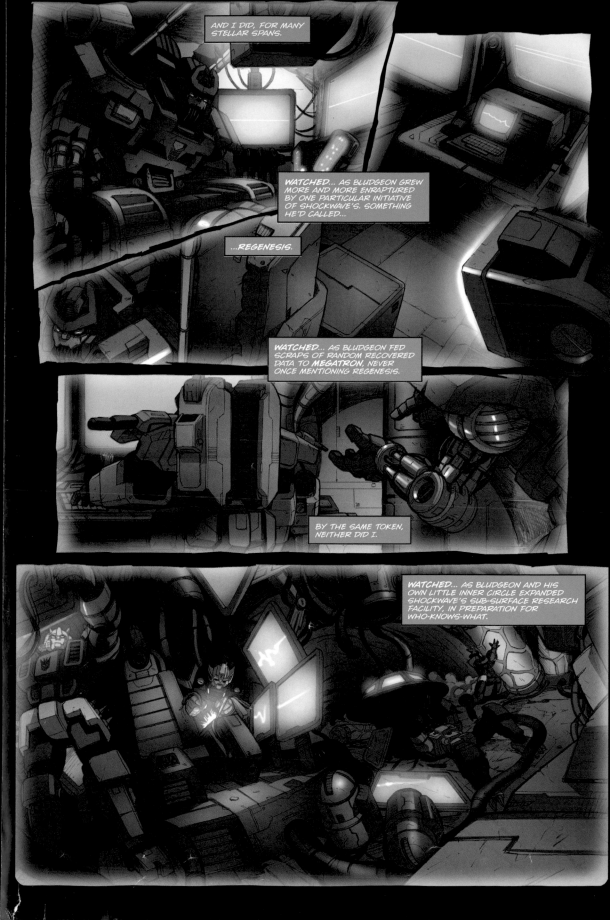

AND I DID, FOR MANY STELLAR SPANS.

WATCHED... AS BLUDGEON GREW MORE AND MORE ENRAPTURED BY ONE PARTICULAR INITIATIVE OF SHOCKWAVE'S. SOMETHING HE'D CALLED...

...REGENESIS.

WATCHED... AS BLUDGEON FED SCRAPS OF RANDOM RECOVERED DATA TO **MEGATRON**, NEVER ONCE MENTIONING REGENESIS.

BY THE SAME TOKEN, NEITHER DID I.

WATCHED... AS BLUDGEON AND HIS OWN LITTLE INNER CIRCLE EXPANDED SHOCKWAVE'S SUB-SURFACE RESEARCH FACILITY, IN PREPARATION FOR WHO-KNOWS-WHAT.

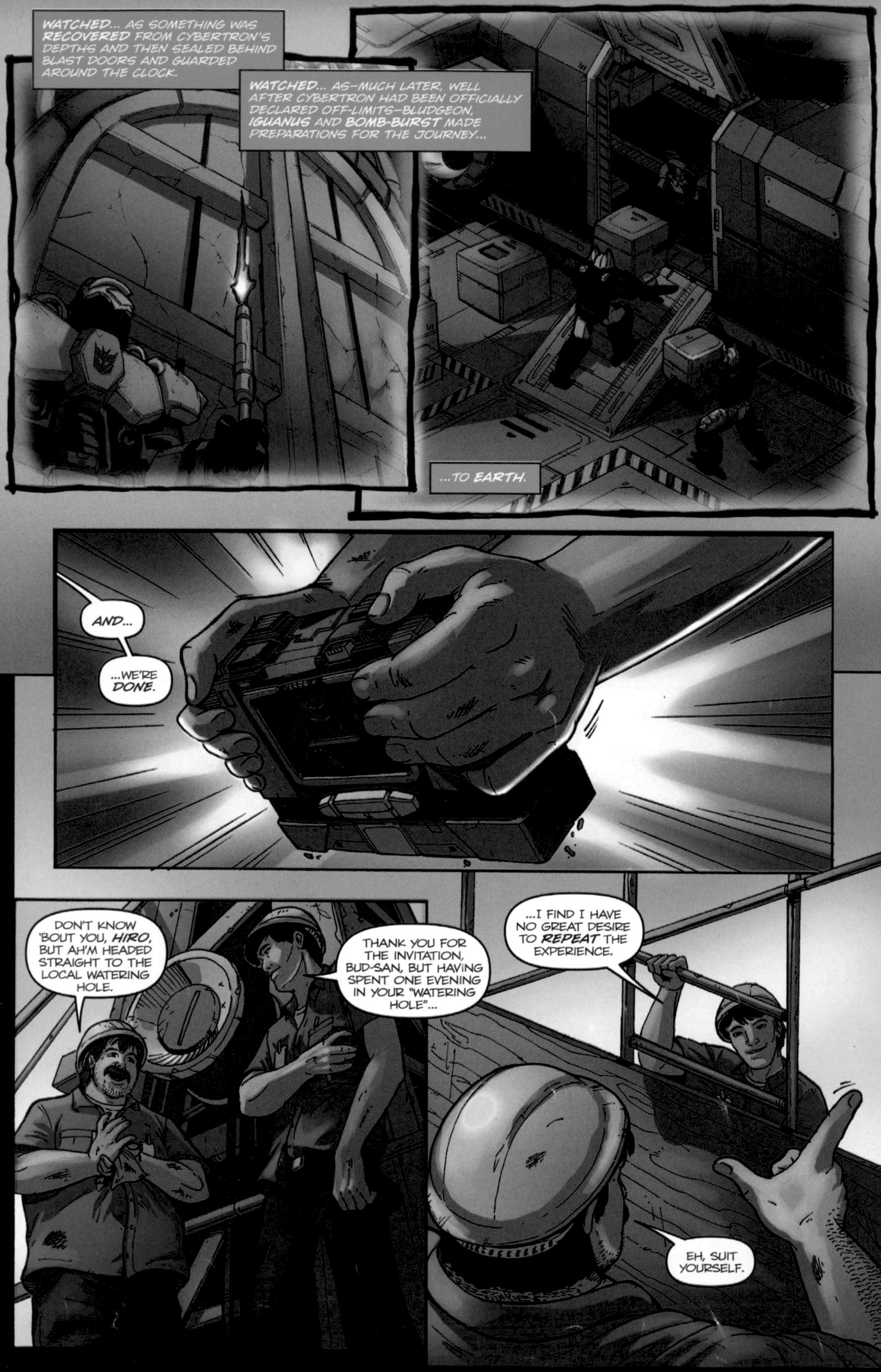
WATCHED... AS SOMETHING WAS RECOVERED FROM CYBERTRON'S DEPTHS AND THEN SEALED BEHIND BLAST DOORS AND GUARDED AROUND THE CLOCK.
WATCHED... AS—MUCH LATER, WELL AFTER CYBERTRON HAD BEEN OFFICIALLY DECLARED OFF-LIMITS—BLUDGEON, IGUANUS AND BOMB-BURST MADE PREPARATIONS FOR THE JOURNEY...
...TO EARTH.
AND...
...WE'RE DONE.
DON'T KNOW 'BOUT YOU, HIRO, BUT AH'M HEADED STRAIGHT TO THE LOCAL WATERING HOLE.
THANK YOU FOR THE INVITATION, BUD-SAN, BUT HAVING SPENT ONE EVENING IN YOUR "WATERING HOLE"...
...I FIND I HAVE NO GREAT DESIRE TO REPEAT THE EXPERIENCE.
EH, SUIT YOURSELF.

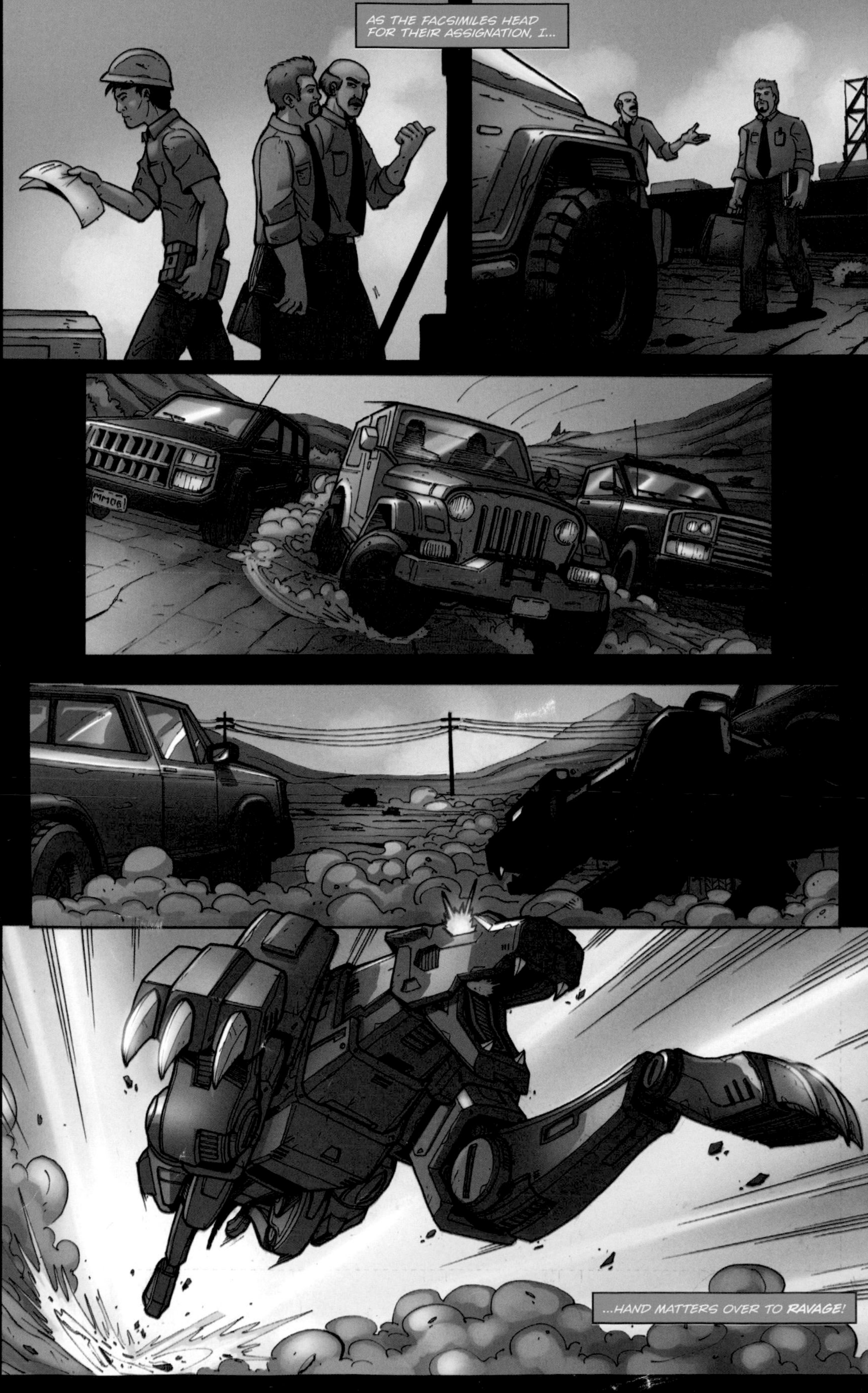
AS THE FACSIMILES HEAD FOR THEIR ASSIGNATION, I...
MM06
...HAND MATTERS OVER TO RAVAGE!

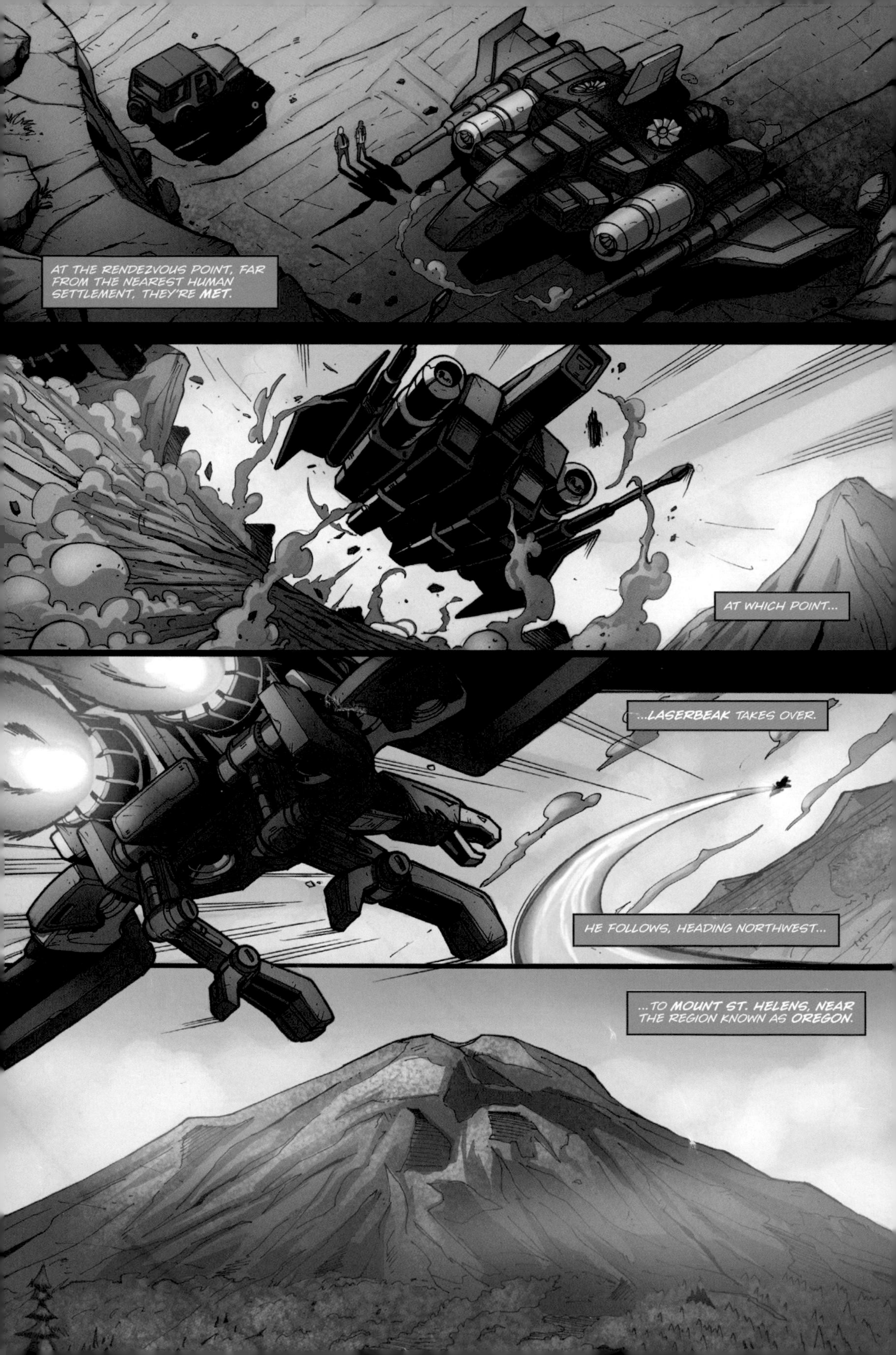
AT THE RENDEZVOUS POINT, FAR FROM THE NEAREST HUMAN SETTLEMENT, THEY'RE **MET**.
AT WHICH POINT...
...**LASERBEAK** TAKES OVER.
HE FOLLOWS, HEADING NORTHWEST...
...TO **MOUNT ST. HELENS**, NEAR THE REGION KNOWN AS **OREGON**.

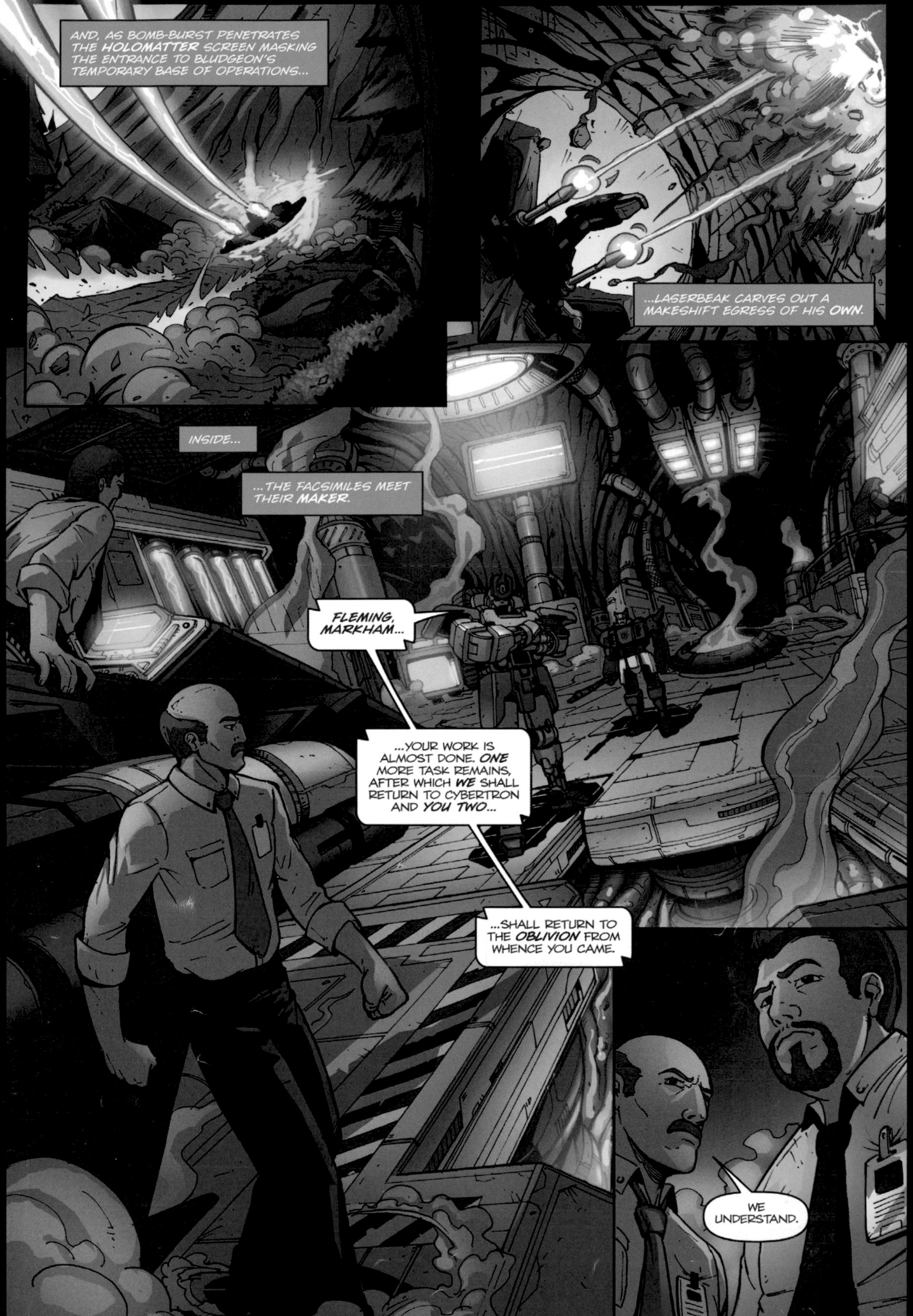
AND, AS BOMB-BURST PENETRATES THE HOLOMATTER SCREEN MASKING THE ENTRANCE TO BLUDGEON'S TEMPORARY BASE OF OPERATIONS...
...LASERBEAK CARVES OUT A MAKESHIFT EGRESS OF HIS OWN.
INSIDE...
...THE FACSIMILES MEET THEIR MAKER.
FLEMING, MARKHAM...
...YOUR WORK IS ALMOST DONE. ONE MORE TASK REMAINS, AFTER WHICH WE SHALL RETURN TO CYBERTRON AND YOU TWO...
...SHALL RETURN TO THE OBLIVION FROM WHENCE YOU CAME.
WE UNDERSTAND.

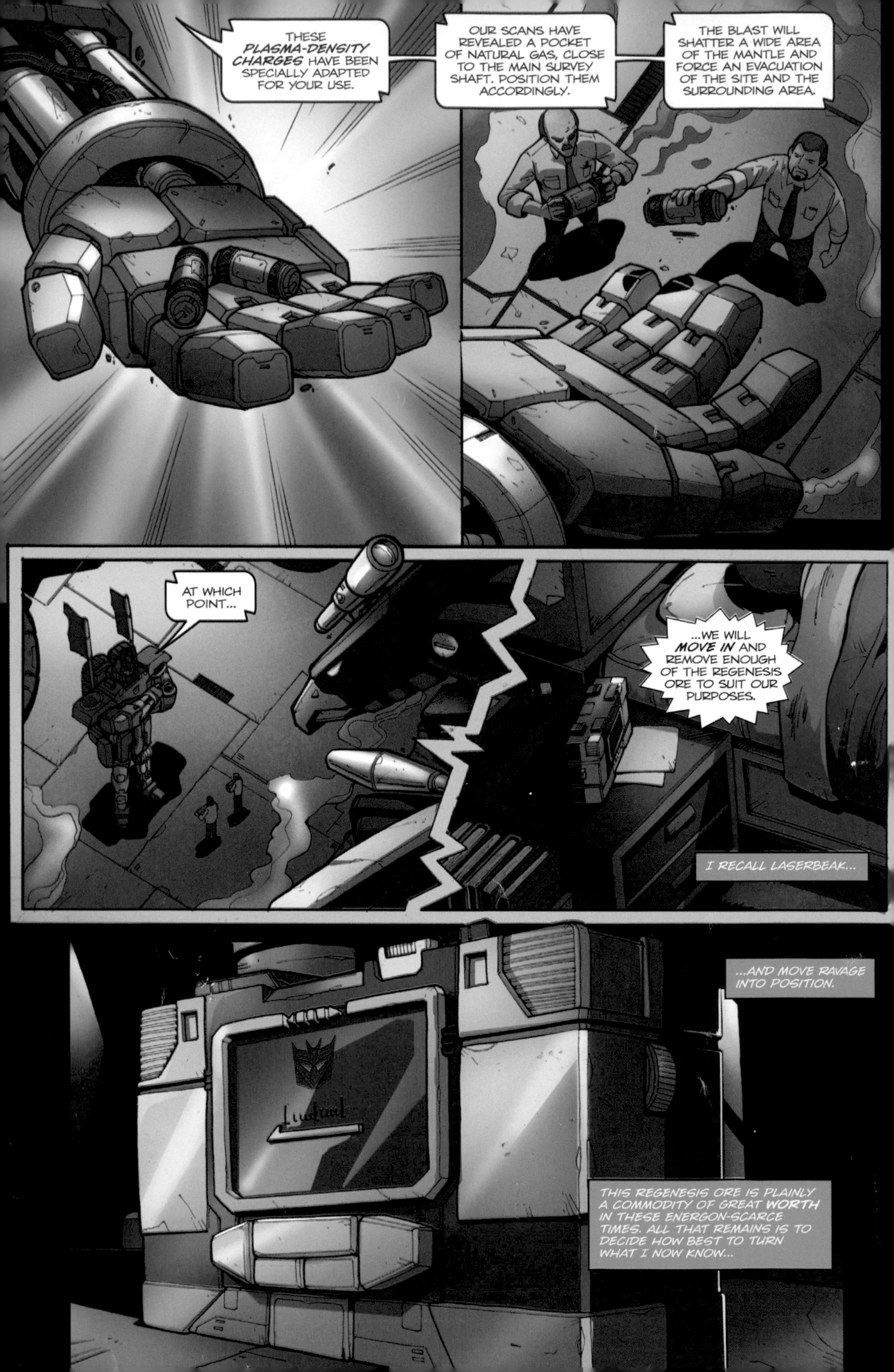
THESE PLASMA-DENSITY CHARGES HAVE BEEN SPECIALLY ADAPTED FOR YOUR USE.
OUR SCANS HAVE REVEALED A POCKET OF NATURAL GAS, CLOSE TO THE MAIN SURVEY SHAFT. POSITION THEM ACCORDINGLY.
THE BLAST WILL SHATTER A WIDE AREA OF THE MANTLE AND FORCE AN EVACUATION OF THE SITE AND THE SURROUNDING AREA.
AT WHICH POINT...
...WE WILL MOVE IN AND REMOVE ENOUGH OF THE REGENESIS ORE TO SUIT OUR PURPOSES.
I RECALL LASERBEAK...
...AND MOVE RAVAGE INTO POSITION.
THIS REGENESIS ORE IS PLAINLY A COMMODITY OF GREAT WORTH IN THESE ENERGON-SCARCE TIMES. ALL THAT REMAINS IS TO DECIDE HOW BEST TO TURN WHAT I NOW KNOW...

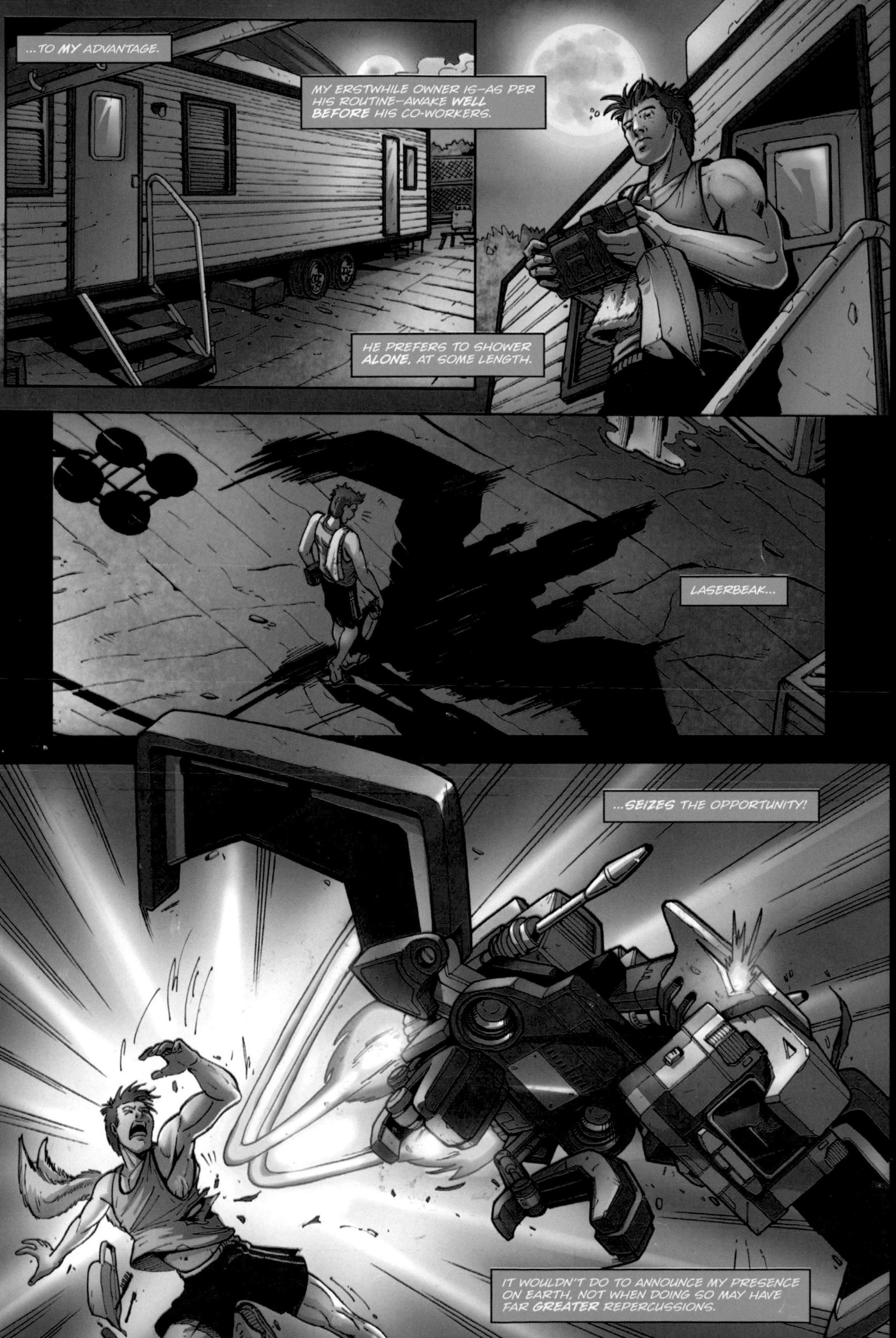
...TO MY ADVANTAGE.
MY ERSTWHILE OWNER IS—AS PER HIS ROUTINE—AWAKE WELL BEFORE HIS CO-WORKERS.
HE PREFERS TO SHOWER ALONE, AT SOME LENGTH.
LASERBEAK...
...SEIZES THE OPPORTUNITY!
IT WOULDN'T DO TO ANNOUNCE MY PRESENCE ON EARTH, NOT WHEN DOING SO MAY HAVE FAR GREATER REPERCUSSIONS.

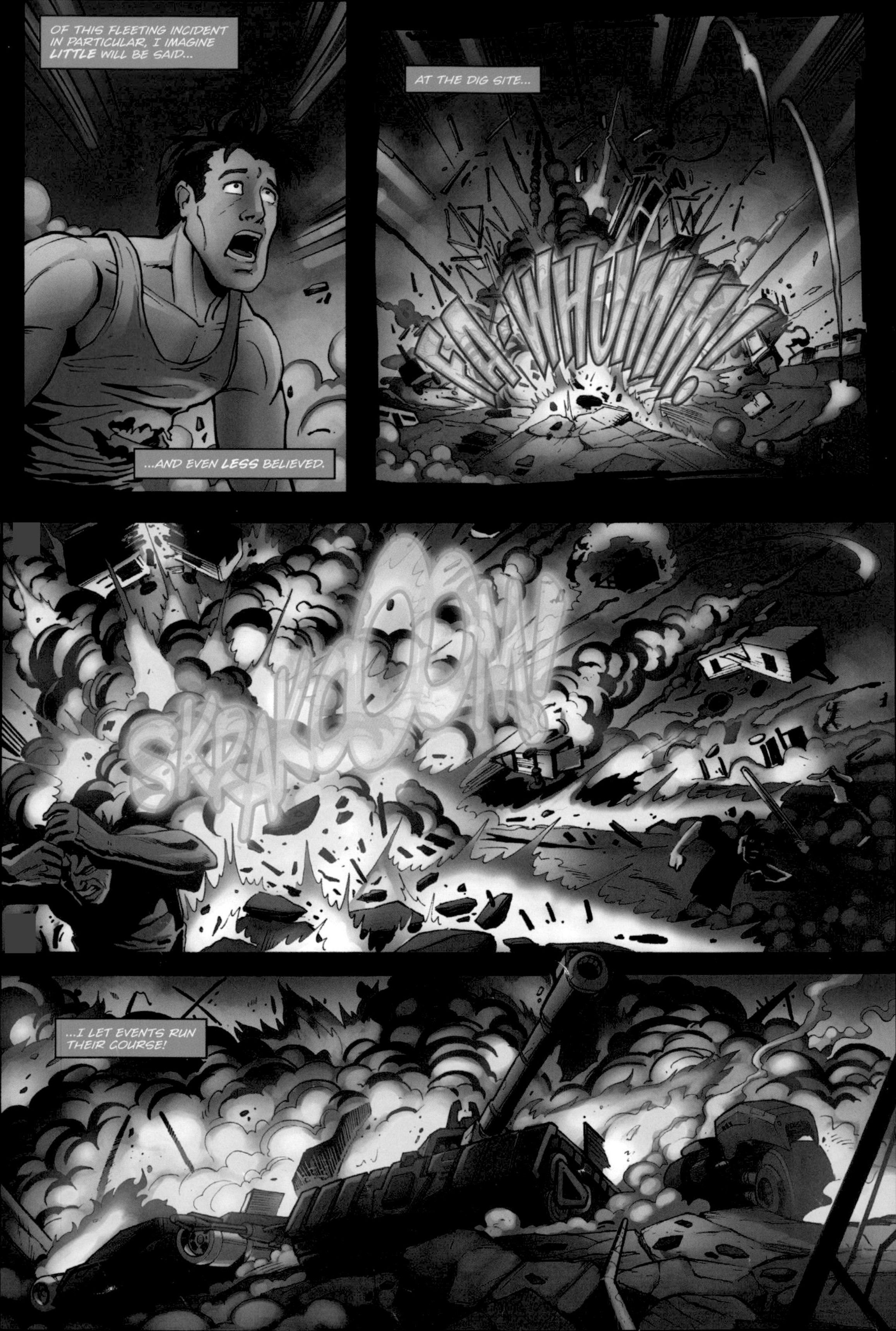

OF THIS FLEETING INCIDENT IN PARTICULAR, I IMAGINE LITTLE WILL BE SAID...
...AND EVEN LESS BELIEVED.
AT THE DIG SITE...
CHA-WHUMM!
SKRAKOOOM!
...I LET EVENTS RUN THEIR COURSE!

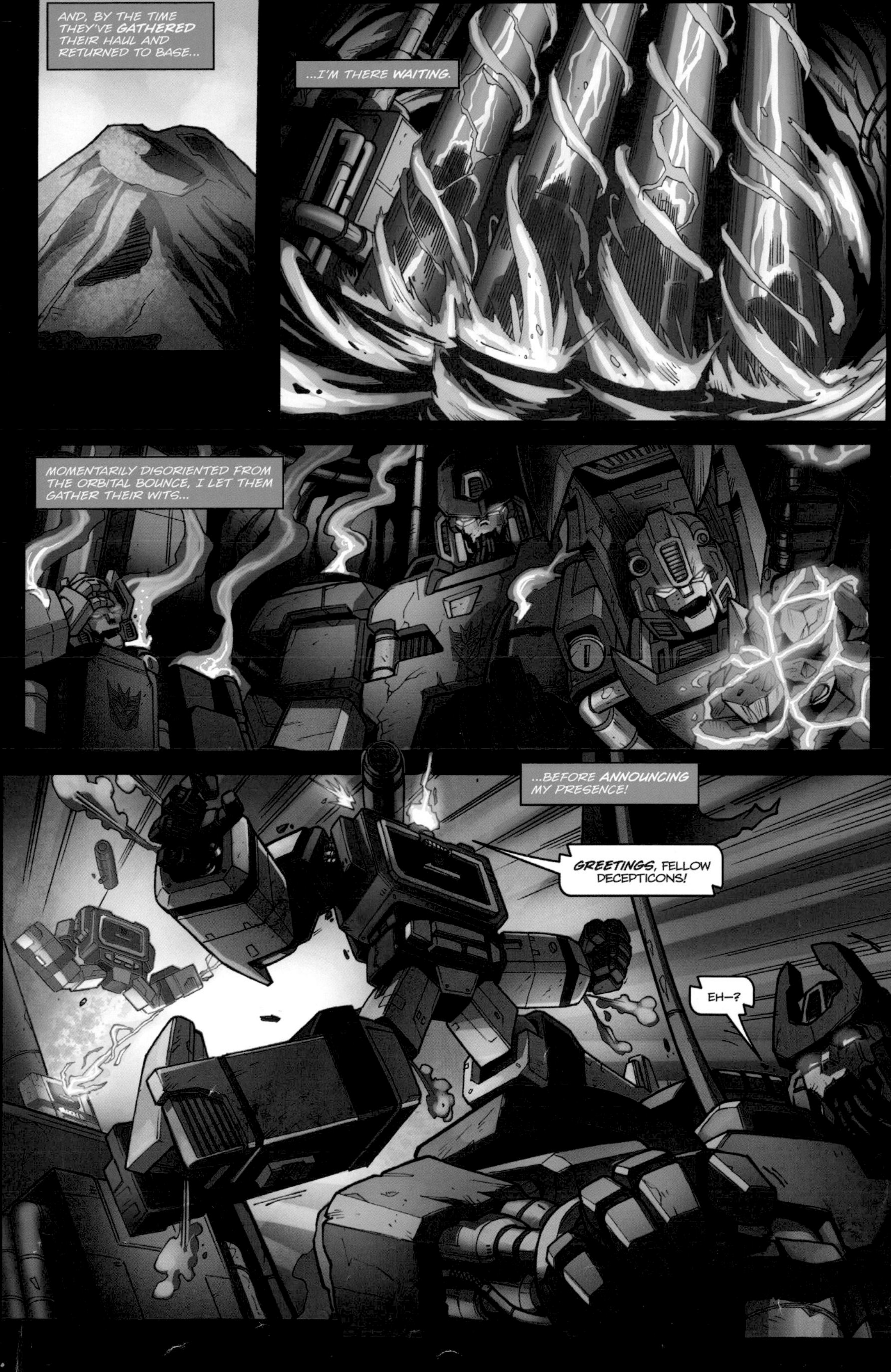
AND, BY THE TIME THEY'VE GATHERED THEIR HAUL AND RETURNED TO BASE...
...I'M THERE WAITING.
MOMENTARILY DISORIENTED FROM THE ORBITAL BOUNCE, I LET THEM GATHER THEIR WITS...
...BEFORE ANNOUNCING MY PRESENCE!
GREETINGS, FELLOW DECEPTICONS!
EH–?

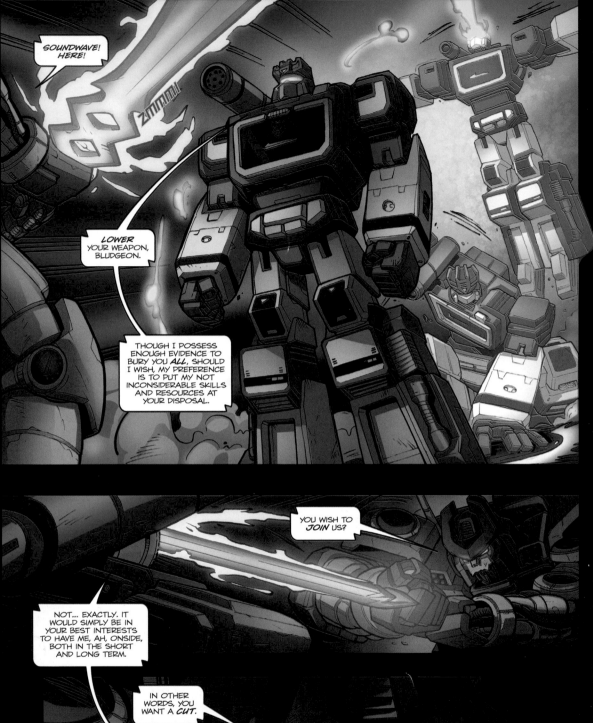

SOUNDWAVE! HERE!

LOWER YOUR WEAPON, BLUDGEON.

THOUGH I POSSESS ENOUGH EVIDENCE TO BURY YOU *ALL*, SHOULD I WISH, MY PREFERENCE IS TO PUT MY NOT INCONSIDERABLE SKILLS AND RESOURCES AT YOUR DISPOSAL.

YOU WISH TO *JOIN* US?

NOT... EXACTLY. IT WOULD SIMPLY BE IN YOUR BEST INTERESTS TO HAVE ME, AH, ONSIDE, BOTH IN THE SHORT AND LONG TERM.

IN OTHER WORDS, YOU WANT A *CUT*.

A CRUDE BUT SUCCINT SUMMATION.

SOUNDWAVE... YOU ARE A *FOOL!*

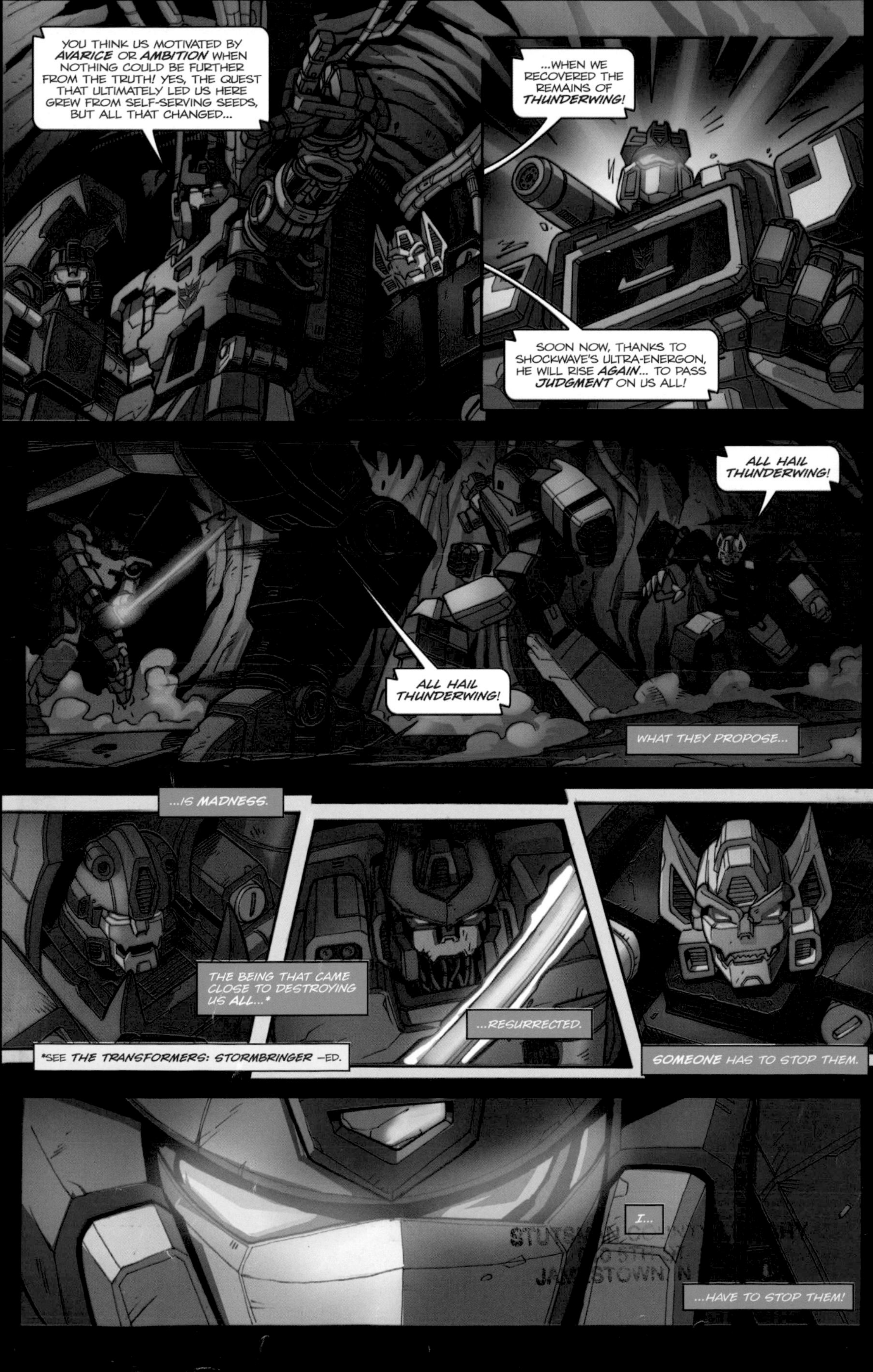

YOU THINK US MOTIVATED BY AVARICE OR AMBITION WHEN NOTHING COULD BE FURTHER FROM THE TRUTH! YES, THE QUEST THAT ULTIMATELY LED US HERE GREW FROM SELF-SERVING SEEDS, BUT ALL THAT CHANGED...
...WHEN WE RECOVERED THE REMAINS OF THUNDERWING!
SOON NOW, THANKS TO SHOCKWAVE'S ULTRA-ENERGON, HE WILL RISE AGAIN... TO PASS JUDGMENT ON US ALL!
ALL HAIL THUNDERWING!
ALL HAIL THUNDERWING!
WHAT THEY PROPOSE...
...IS MADNESS.
THE BEING THAT CAME CLOSE TO DESTROYING US ALL...*
*SEE THE TRANSFORMERS: STORMBRINGER —ED.
...RESURRECTED.
SOMEONE HAS TO STOP THEM.
I...
...HAVE TO STOP THEM!

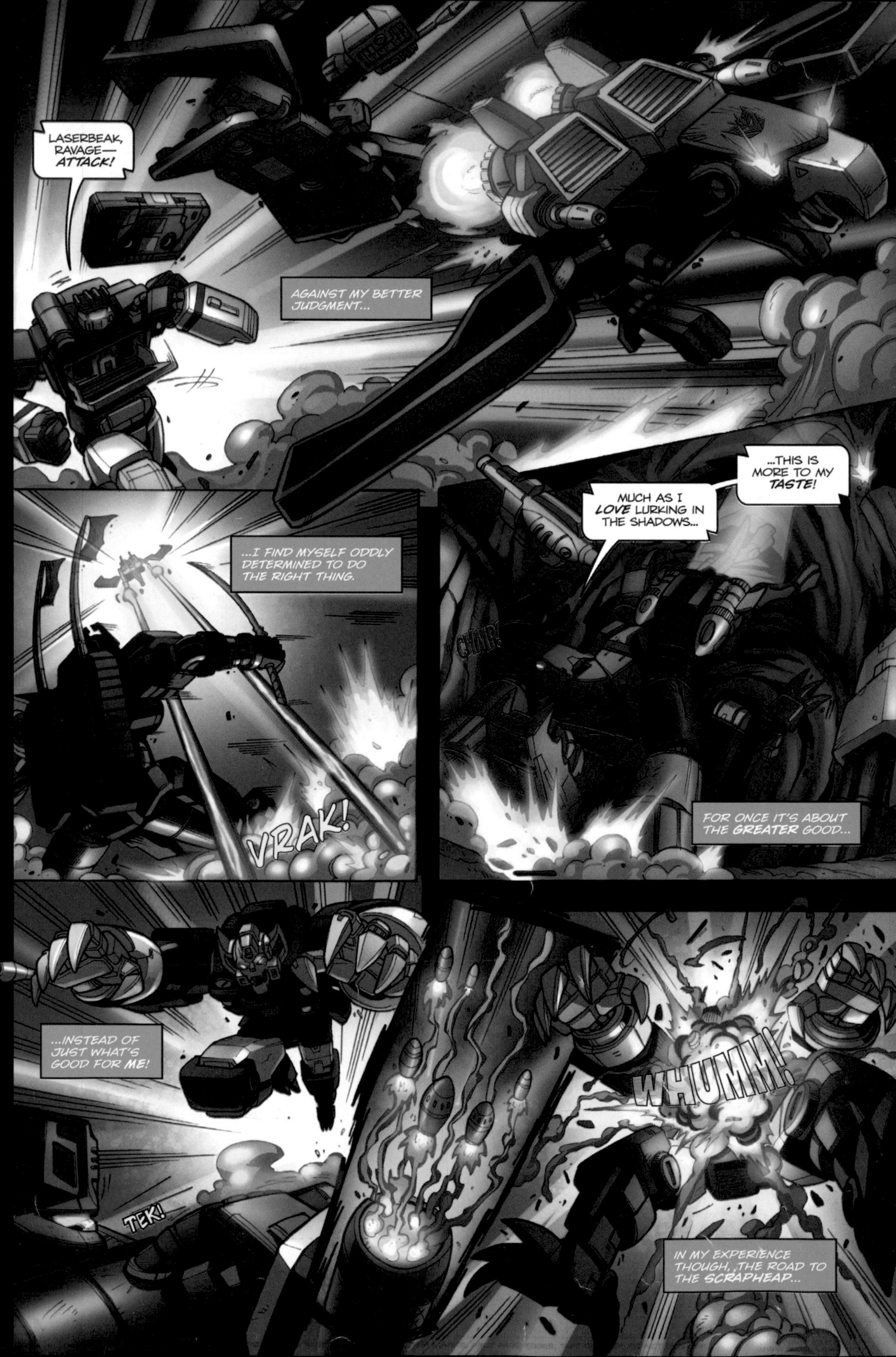
LASERBEAK, RAVAGE— ATTACK!
AGAINST MY BETTER JUDGMENT...
...I FIND MYSELF ODDLY DETERMINED TO DO THE RIGHT THING.
VRAK!
MUCH AS I LOVE LURKING IN THE SHADOWS...
...THIS IS MORE TO MY TASTE!
FOR ONCE IT'S ABOUT THE GREATER GOOD...
...INSTEAD OF JUST WHAT'S GOOD FOR ME!
TEK!
WHUMM!
IN MY EXPERIENCE THOUGH, THE ROAD TO THE SCRAPHEAP...

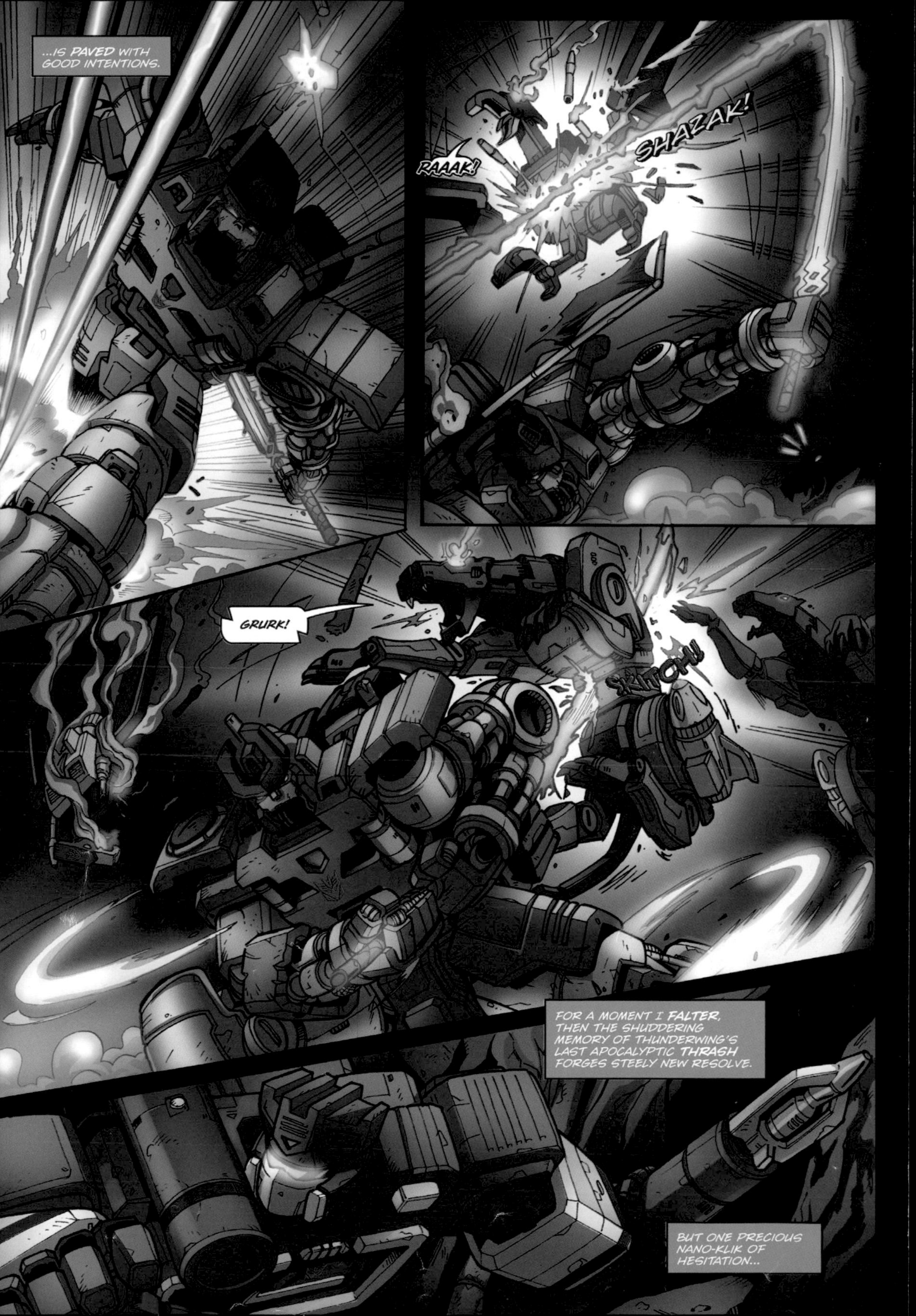
...IS PAVED WITH GOOD INTENTIONS.
RAAAK!
SHAZAK!
GRURK!
SKITCH!
FOR A MOMENT I FALTER, THEN THE SHUDDERING MEMORY OF THUNDERWING'S LAST APOCALYPTIC THRASH FORGES STEELY NEW RESOLVE.
BUT ONE PRECIOUS NANO-KLIK OF HESITATION...

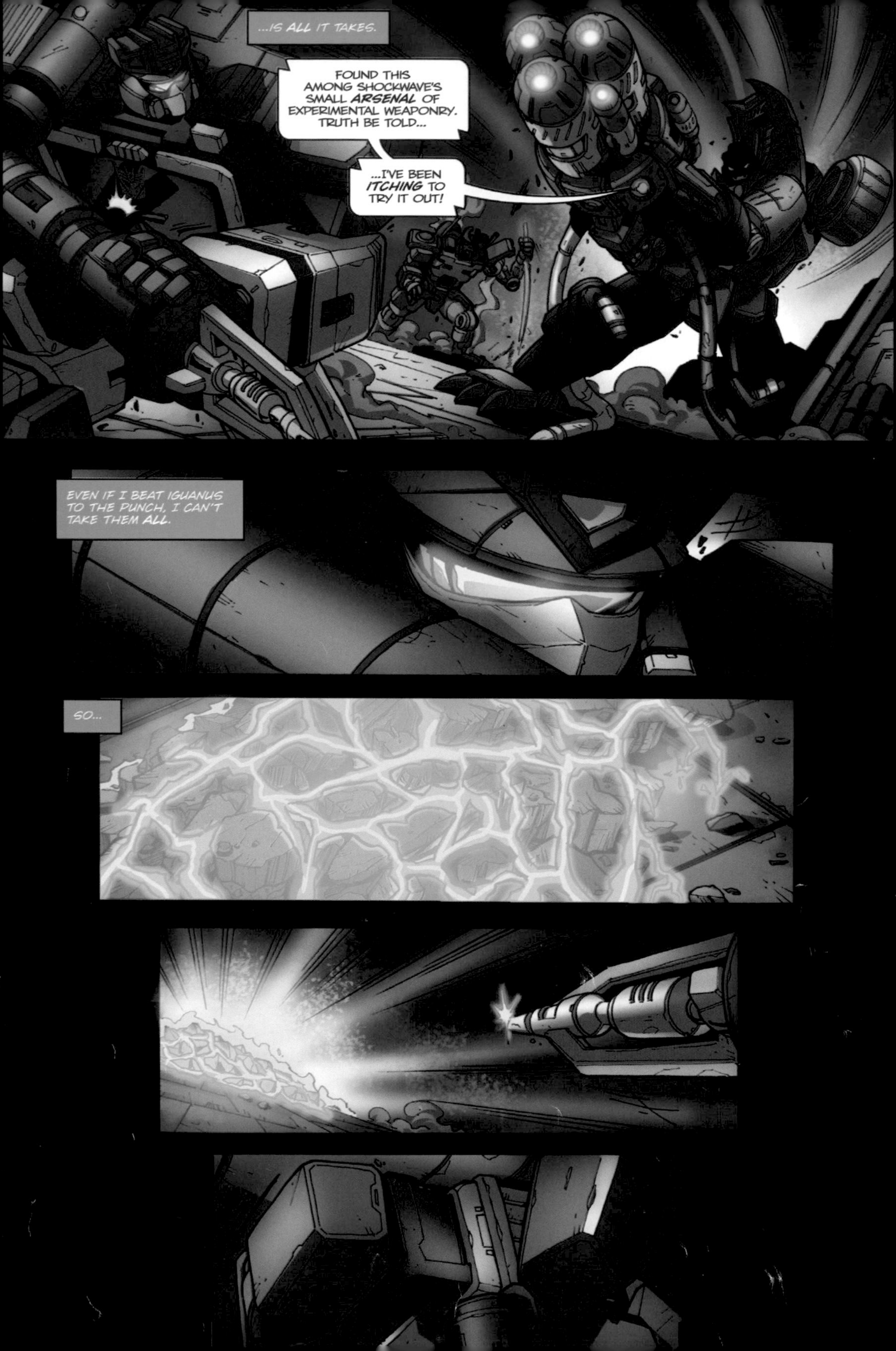
...IS ALL IT TAKES.
FOUND THIS AMONG SHOCKWAVE'S SMALL ARSENAL OF EXPERIMENTAL WEAPONRY. TRUTH BE TOLD...
...I'VE BEEN ITCHING TO TRY IT OUT!
EVEN IF I BEAT IGUANUS TO THE PUNCH, I CAN'T TAKE THEM ALL.
SO...

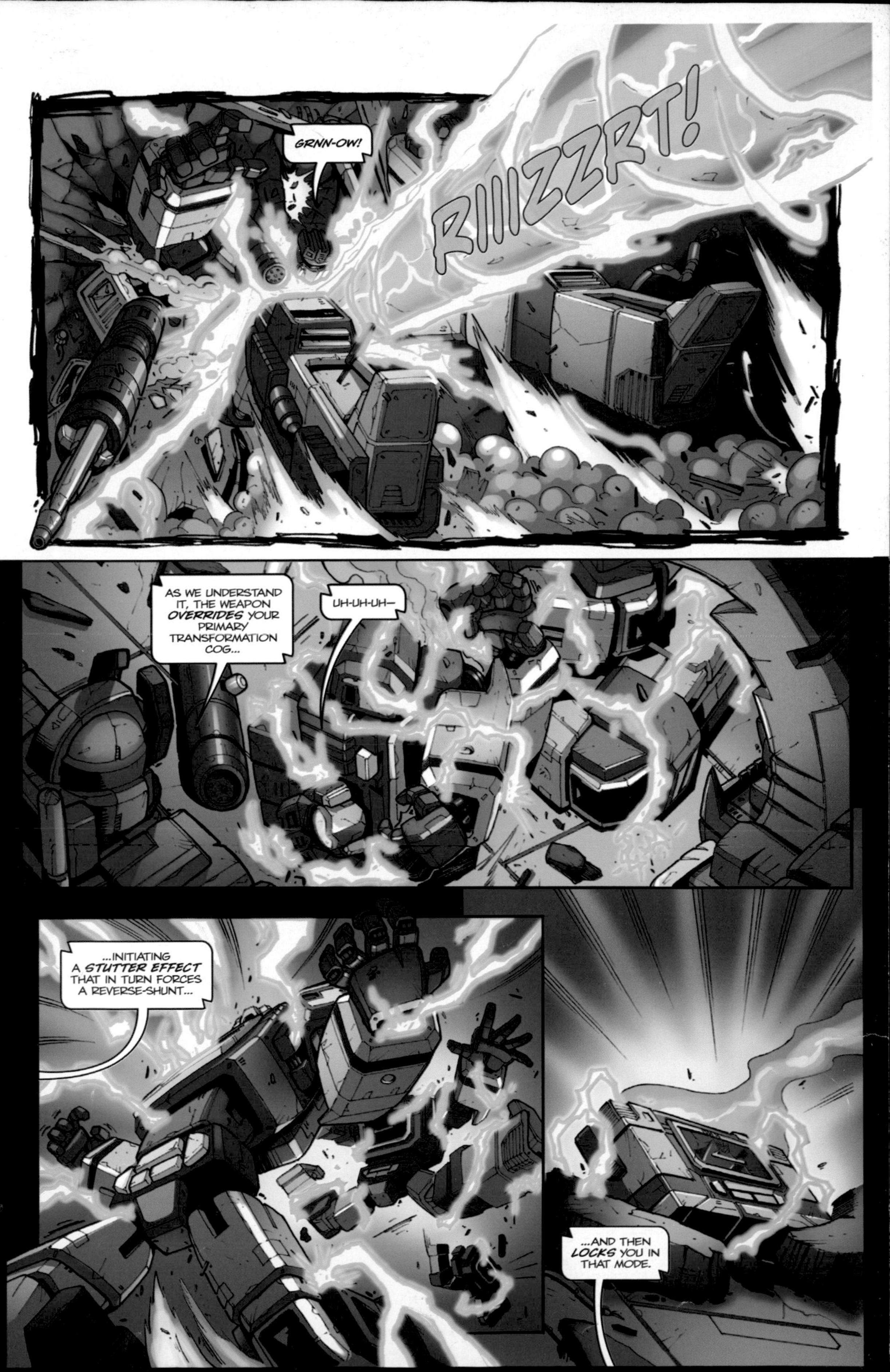
GRNN-OW!
RIIIZZZRT!
AS WE UNDERSTAND IT, THE WEAPON OVERRIDES YOUR PRIMARY TRANSFORMATION COG...
UH-UH-UH—
...INITIATING A STUTTER EFFECT THAT IN TURN FORCES A REVERSE-SHUNT...
...AND THEN LOCKS YOU IN THAT MODE.

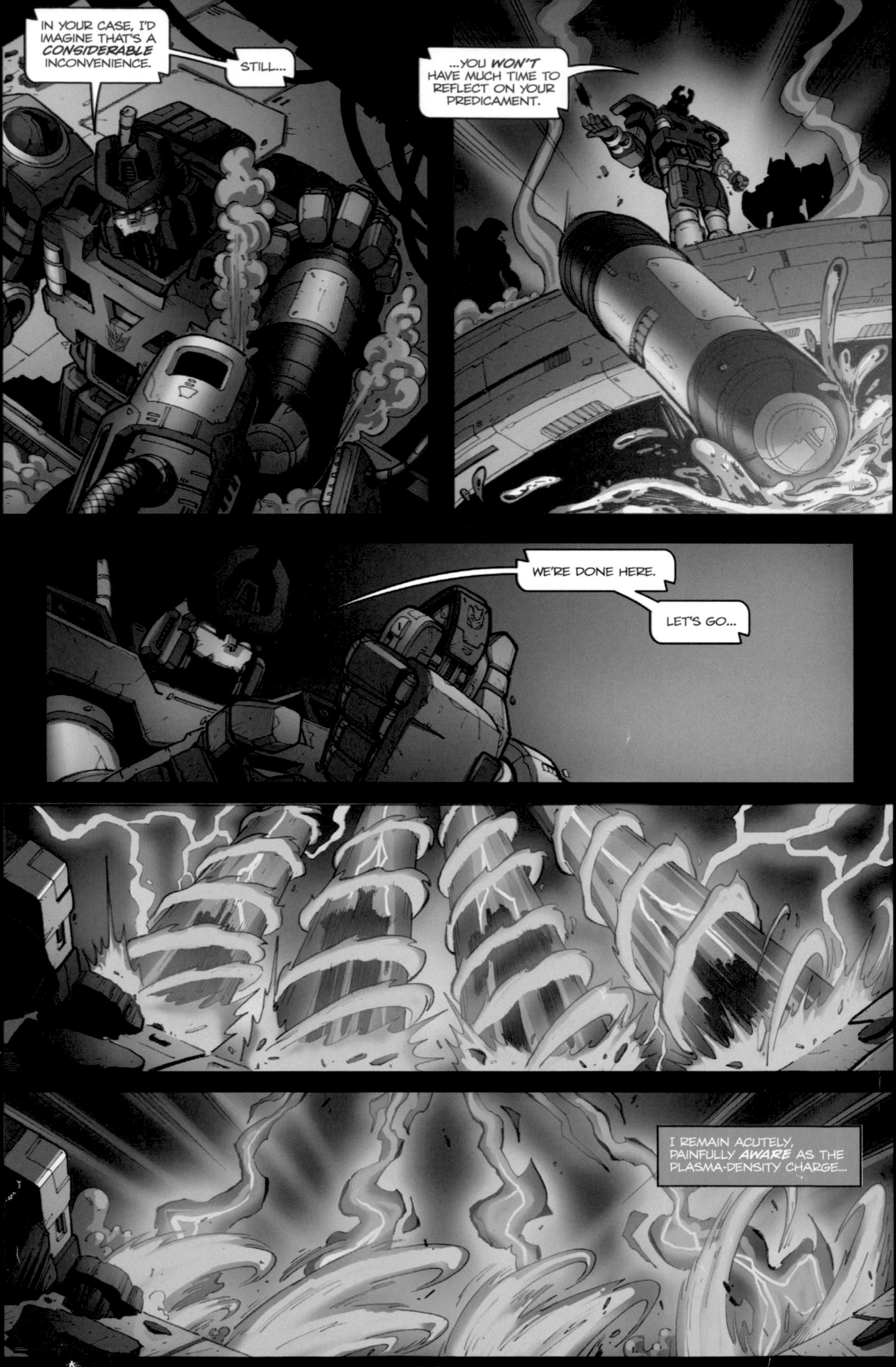
IN YOUR CASE, I'D IMAGINE THAT'S A CONSIDERABLE INCONVENIENCE.
STILL...
...YOU WON'T HAVE MUCH TIME TO REFLECT ON YOUR PREDICAMENT.
WE'RE DONE HERE.
LET'S GO...
I REMAIN ACUTELY, PAINFULLY AWARE AS THE PLASMA-DENSITY CHARGE...

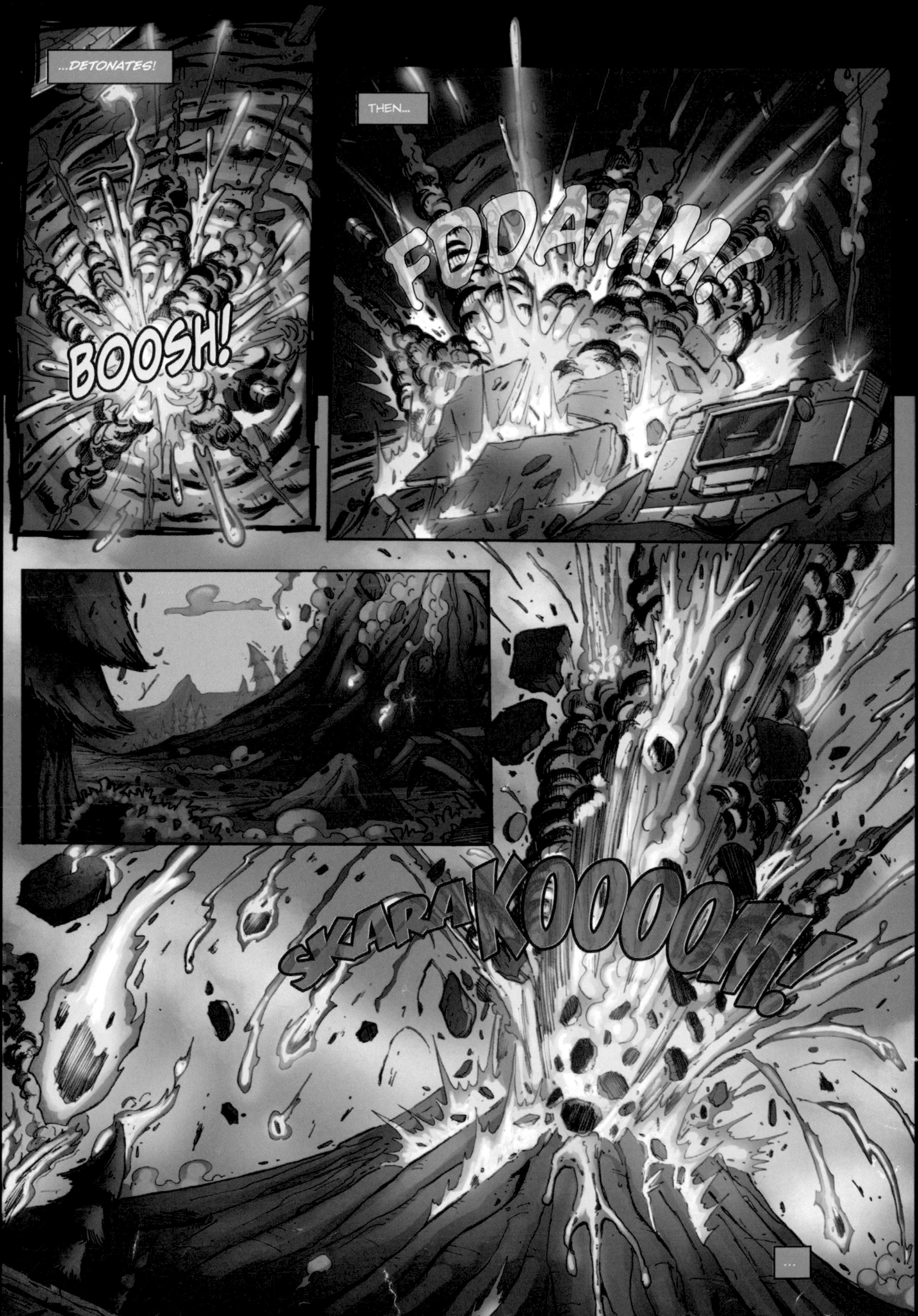
...DETONATES!
BOOSH!
THEN...
FODAMM!!
SKARAKOOOOM!
...

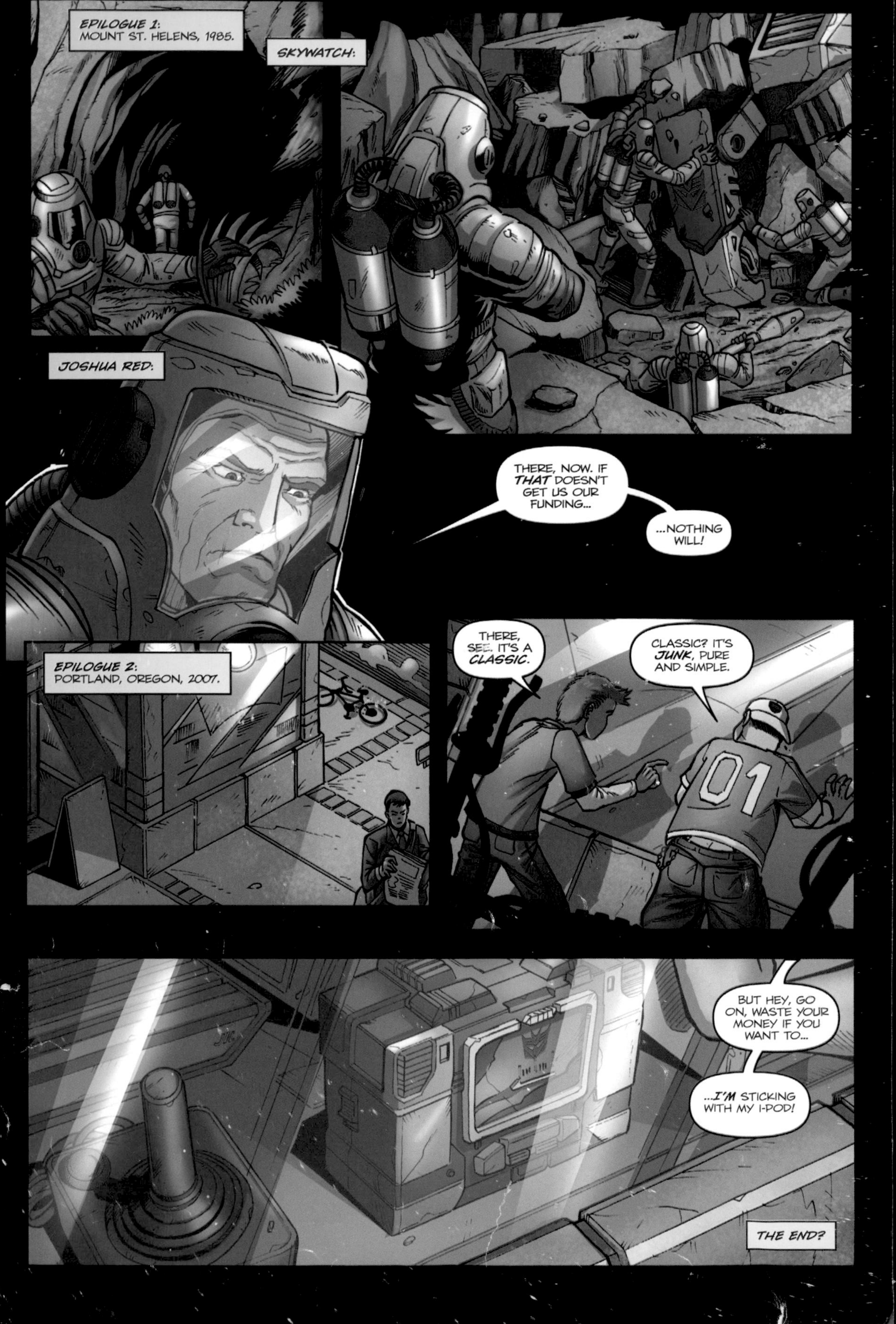
EPILOGUE 1:
MOUNT ST. HELENS, 1985.
SKYWATCH:
JOSHUA RED:
THERE, NOW. IF THAT DOESN'T GET US OUR FUNDING...
...NOTHING WILL!
EPILOGUE 2:
PORTLAND, OREGON, 2007.
THERE, SEE. IT'S A CLASSIC.
CLASSIC? IT'S JUNK, PURE AND SIMPLE.
01
BUT HEY, GO ON, WASTE YOUR MONEY IF YOU WANT TO...
...I'M STICKING WITH MY I-POD!
THE END?